LIN OLIVER

THE FANTASTIC FRAME

For Marsha Norman, my cherished
New York sister—LO

To my parents, Susanne, Rudy, Matthew, and Cheryl,
with all my love, thank you!—SK

W

PENGUIN WORKSHOP
An Imprint of Penguin Random House LLC, New York

Text copyright © 2016 by Lin Oliver. Illustrations copyright © 2016 by
Samantha Kallis. All rights reserved. Previously published in hardcover in 2016
by Grosset & Dunlap. This paperback edition published in 2019 by Penguin Workshop, an
imprint of Penguin Random House LLC, New York. PENGUIN and PENGUIN WORKSHOP
are trademarks of Penguin Books Ltd, and the W colophon is a registered trademark of
Penguin Random House LLC. Manufactured in China.

Visit us online at www.penguinrandomhouse.com.

Library of Congress Control Number: 2016029287

ISBN 9780448480909 | 10 9 8 7 6 5 4 3 2 1

THE FANTASTIC FRAME

Beware! Shadows in the Night

BY **LIN OLIVER**

ILLUSTRATED BY
SAMANTHA KALLIS

Penguin Workshop

PROLOGUE

Hello there. It's Tiger Brooks. That's right, I'm the guy who travels into the fantastic frame. I bet you remember me. I don't mean to sound like I'm bragging. It's not like I think I'm all that great or anything. I just know that it's hard to forget a person who gets sucked into a painting and only has an hour to get out.

You don't meet someone like that every day.

This little habit I have of time traveling

into paintings began when my friend Luna Lopez and I discovered the fantastic frame. It hangs on the living room wall in the old run-down house, of our neighbor Viola Dots. At first, Luna and I thought it was nothing but a golden frame with carved animals and a clock on the front. We didn't know about the hour of power. That's when the clock on the frame strikes four and the painting inside opens up and sucks you in.

But we sure found out about that hour of power in a hurry!

If you ask me, I think Chives should have warned us. He's Viola's butler who happens to be an orange pig. But being a pig is no excuse, because he can talk.

Chives knew that Viola's son, David, disappeared into the frame fifty years ago and never returned. The only thing she got back was pudgy Chives, who came flying straight out of some old pig painting wearing a top hat and a bowtie and has been living with her ever since.

Mrs. Dots is a real grump, but Luna and I feel sorry for her, anyway. She misses her son, David, a lot, which is why we decided to help her. Every time Viola finishes a new painting for the frame, she asks us to go inside and look for David. She's never been able to go inside a painting herself. She always gets spit out. Maybe adults aren't allowed in. Or maybe it's just the grumpy adults who aren't allowed in.

Once we're inside the painting, Luna and I have to watch the time carefully, because if we're not back at exactly the same spot in the painting at five o'clock, then we could be stuck there forever.

Now David, he really doesn't seem to mind being stuck inside paintings. I have to admit, sometimes it doesn't seem so bad to me, either. I wouldn't have to watch my annoying little sister, Maggie, chew with her mouth open. I wouldn't have to roll my socks into pairs and put them away in my sock drawer. And I wouldn't have to learn how to do subtraction word problems.

On the other hand, I'd miss my comfy bed and my dad's spaghetti sauce. Although those hot dogs and giant pretzels off the street cart in New York sure were delicious. But wait. I'm getting ahead of myself. You don't even know about New York yet and the weird thing that happened there. I'm talking weird with a capital *W*.

If you're interested, keep reading. You'll find out all about it.

CHAPTER 1

Luna and I stood on our driveway after school, staring at my new invention.

"What do you think I should call it?" I asked her.

Luna walked around in a circle. She still had on the cool superhero cape she had worn to school that day. She looked at the contraption in front of her and scratched her head.

"You could call it a *thingamajig*," she suggested. "That's got a nice ring to it."

"But *thingamajig* doesn't tell you what it does," I said.

"Good point, Tiger. By the way, what *does* it do?"

It was Transportation Week at school. Everyone in our class had to do an oral report about a means of transportation. Luna chose to do hers on flying through the sky like Moon Girl. That's the superhero name she's given herself. She picked it because "Luna" means *moon* in Spanish. Too bad her parents didn't name her something cool like Shark or Crusher. Personally, I'd take Shark Girl or the Crusher over Moon Girl any day.

Even though Luna had gone to all the trouble of making herself a Moon Girl cape, our teacher, Ms. Warner, wasn't impressed. She said flying around on air currents was only a means of transportation for comic book characters. And everyone knows they don't actually exist.

The report Ms. Warner loved was Andrew Hogan's on electric cars. She said it was outstanding, the best in the class. But then, she hadn't seen mine yet. Mine was going to knock her shoes *and* socks off. That's because I decided that instead of doing a report, I'd invent my own means of transportation. And I did.

"I got the idea for my invention yesterday," I explained to Luna, "when I was riding my bike. I got really hungry and I thought—wouldn't it be great to have a snack any time you want one? Even on a bike. So I invented this . . . uh . . . thingamajig!"

"Tiger, can I just point out one thing?" Luna said. "The thingamajig isn't a bike."

"Yeah, I noticed that," I answered. "But I

wasn't about to experiment with my brand-new bike. So I used my little sister's pink princess scooter instead."

"Uh-oh. Something tells me Maggie's not going to like that."

"She won't care. She's totally over the princess thing."

"Right. That's why she wore a diamond crown to preschool this morning. And carried a light-up wand."

"I couldn't help it," I explained. "I *had* to borrow her scooter. Don't tell, but I kind of borrowed my dad's cooler, too. See, I attached it to the scooter. The cooler gives you a nice place to sit while you're scooting and keeps your butt cool at the same time."

"That's important," Luna said. "You don't want to get your butt all overheated."

We both cracked up at that. It's nice to have a friend who makes you laugh.

"Here's the great part about my invention," I went on. "If you get hungry when you're scooting around, all you have to do is flip open the cooler and get yourself a snack. Snack and scoot, it's the perfect combo."

"That's it!" Luna said. "You just gave your invention a name. The Snack 'N' Scoot."

"Hmmmmm . . . The Snack 'N' Scoot." I rolled the words around in my mouth. They sounded pretty good.

"Let's try it out," I said.

"We promised Viola we'd be at her house before four o'clock," Luna reminded me. "We can't be late for the hour of power."

"We have a few minutes until then," I

told her. "Let's just take one quick spin."

I got on first and took off down the sidewalk. When I got to Viola's house, I slowed down and looked up the overgrown path to her crumbling blue house. It's so old and run-down, people on our block think it's haunted. Luna and I are the only people in the neighborhood who have ever been inside.

I noticed Chives peeking out from behind the ragged red velvet curtain. He always keeps himself hidden. Viola doesn't want anyone to know that she has a talking orange pig for a butler. I waved to him. He took a gold watch out of his vest pocket and pointed to it with his hoof.

I gave him a thumbs-up, to let him know we'd be there on time, and rode back to Luna.

As she was getting on the Snack 'N' Scoot to take her turn, my dad's car pulled into the driveway. He was bringing my sister home from preschool. Maggie stuck her head out the car window.

"Hey, Tiger, that's *my* princess scooter," she yelled. "Who said you could take it?"

"Told you," Luna whispered.

"Listen, Maggie." I went to the car and lifted her out of her car seat. "Did I ever tell you what a great little sister you are?"

I plastered a giant smile on my face.

"Put me down, Tiger. I want my scooter back."

"But it's not a scooter anymore," I told her. "Let me introduce you to the Snack 'N' Scoot."

Maggie marched up to the scooter and looked it right in the handlebars.

"I'm *not* happy to meet you," she said.

"Well, now, Tiger, it seems that you also took my cooler," my dad said. "That's the one we take to the beach. I don't remember you asking permission to use it."

"Sorry, Dad," I said, "but it's for my school project."

"I don't care what it's for," he said. "You can't just take things without asking. I want you to return the cooler to the garage and the scooter to Maggie."

"But, Dad!" I cried. "I have to do my transportation oral report tomorrow. And the Snack 'N' Scoot is my report."

"Not anymore it isn't," he said. "Luna, I'm afraid Tiger can't play now. He's got to come inside and write his report. A real report this time."

He took Maggie's hand and they walked up the driveway to the house.

"And you better not forget to put my purple basket back on," Maggie called over her shoulder. "It has magical princess powers."

I was so mad, I wanted to scream.

"My dad doesn't understand anything about my inventions," I told Luna. "He wants me to do a plain old regular report. Now I'll have to write a whole bunch of paragraphs and look up words and stuff."

"The worst part is that we're not going to

be able to go to Viola's," Luna said. "We're going to miss the hour of power."

I was so angry, I had forgotten about the painting in the fantastic frame. It opened up at exactly four o'clock, which was only a few minutes away. There was no way I could finish my report before then.

"I don't want to disappoint Viola," I said to Luna. "Maybe we should just go, anyway."

"That would make your dad really mad," Luna said.

I stood there trying to decide what to do, but only for a second. My thoughts were interrupted by Luna's mom, screaming out the top-floor window.

"Luna! Luna!" she called. "Come quickly! You're not going to believe what's happened!"

CHAPTER 2

When she heard her mother's voice, Luna looked so scared. Her dad is a helicopter pilot in the army. I could tell she was worried that something bad had happened to him.

"Mama!" she yelled, running to the window. "What is it? Is it Papa?"

"*Si, mija!*" her mother said. "It's Papa!"

Her mother was crying. I took Luna's hand, to help her prepare for anything.

"He's coming home tonight," her mother

shouted. Then she went from crying to laughing. "Papa just called and he's coming home on leave. He can stay with us the whole weekend!"

Luna burst into tears also. I've heard that people cry when they're happy, but personally, it's never happened to me. I cry when I'm sad or mad or when my mom peels onions. Other than that, my eyes stay pretty dry.

Luna hugged me so hard, I thought I was going to pop.

"I haven't seen my papa in six months," she said. "I am so happy I could dance."

Then she did. She twirled around and around so fast that her cape flared straight out. It looked like Moon Girl was about to take off and fly through the air. Boy, I wished Ms. Warner could have seen that!

"Come upstairs, *mi amor*," Luna's mother called down to her. "We have so much to do to get ready. We're going to make your papa a wonderful fiesta."

"I'll be right there, Mama," Luna called back. She turned to me. "Now neither of us can go to Viola's," she said.

"Mrs. Dots is going to be so sad. We should at least tell her we can't go."

"I'm sure she'll understand," Luna said.

We both knew that wasn't true. Viola

Dots liked to have things her way. She was very good at painting. And very good at bossing Chives around. But understanding someone else's problems—well, that wasn't high on the list of things she was good at. In fact, I had a feeling it might be at the bottom of the list.

"Okay, let's tell her and get it over with," I said. "We'll take the Snack 'N' Scoot for one last ride."

I sat down on the cooler, and Luna got on behind me. We scooted along the sidewalk.

"This is just like riding a motorcycle," Luna said. "Let's see how fast this thing can go. Come on, Tiger. Fly like the wind!"

Luna let out a whoop and we both pushed off as hard as we could. As we sped up to Viola's gate, I turned the handlebars hard to the right. We screeched around the corner and up the path to Viola's house.

The front door opened, and Viola Dots stuck her head out. Her hair looked especially messed up today. I could see why people in the neighborhood thought she was a witch.

"It's about time!" she shouted, her lips pressed into a thin line. "Where have you been?"

Before we could answer, Chives appeared at the door.

"I'll handle this, Madame," he said,

putting a gentle hoof on her shoulder. "After all, I am the doorman. Or should I say—door pig?"

"If you insist, Chives." Viola sighed. "Get them inside quickly. And bring that crazy contraption in, too. Hurry. I don't want to miss the hour of power."

"Mrs. Dots," I began. "About the hour of power. That's why we came to talk to you."

"We're certainly not going to have this conversation here on the porch. Chives, I thought you were bringing that odd vehicle in." She pointed a crooked finger at Luna and me. "You two, follow me. And make it snappy."

She headed into the living room as Chives pulled the Snack 'N' Scoot inside.

"This looks like quite an amusing ride," he said. "Might I try it out? I never get to do anything even the least bit amusing."

"Sure," I said. "Just be careful. It was built for small people, not for big pigs. No offense, Chives."

"None taken, young sir," he said.

"Children!" Viola shouted from the living room. "Have you turned into statues?

I thought I told you to follow me. You're wasting time."

"Madame is particularly excited about this week's painting," Chives said as he threw one of his stubby legs over the cooler. "She says she can feel her son, David, inside it. She is hoping that today will be the day he comes home."

"Today?" Luna asked. She shot me a worried look.

"Yes. She has her poor old heart set on it."

"But, Chives," I said. "We can't go today. That's what we came to tell her."

"Oh my," he said. "Oh my, my, my. I certainly don't want to be there when you tell her that."

Neither did we.

CHAPTER 3

When we walked into the living room, Viola Dots was pacing back and forth. A new painting hung in the fantastic frame.

The painting showed three people sitting in a small restaurant. A blond guy in a white cap was working behind the counter. The lights in the restaurant were bright yellow, but outside, the empty street was dark and full of shadows. Something about the painting made me feel sad and lonely.

"This painting is called *Nighthawks*,"

Viola said. "The original was painted by Edward Hopper, one of the most famous American artists who ever lived."

"Mrs. Dots," I interrupted. "We'd love to learn all about Edward Hopper another time. Today isn't a good day."

"Nonsense, there is no time like the present," she said, barely stopping to take a breath. "As you can see from the clock, we have three minutes before four o'clock. Plenty of time to learn a few things."

"Actually, we don't have plenty of time," Luna said.

Viola waved her wrinkled hand and went on talking.

"This painting," she said, "is of a diner in New York City. A *diner* is a small restaurant. No one knows exactly where it is, but I believe it was somewhere near where I was born. Perhaps that's why I have such a special feeling about it. It brings back so many long-ago memories."

She took a handkerchief out of her sleeve and dabbed at her eyes. I didn't have the heart to interrupt her now.

"The painting was completed in 1942," she went on, "just after the United States entered World War II, a terrible time in our history. I was a small child then. I remember how much I missed my father, who was fighting in the war, far away."

"Speaking of fathers," Luna said. "We came to tell you that mine is coming home today for the weekend."

This seemed to catch Viola's attention.

"Doesn't your father live with you?" she asked.

"He's in the army," Luna answered. "He doesn't get to come home often, but he's coming home tonight."

"Well, then, we'll have to see that you return exactly on time," Mrs. Dots said. "Now, back to Edward Hopper."

"That's just the thing," Luna interrupted. "I can't go. I have to see my papa. I can't take a chance on going into the painting. What if something happens during the hour of power and we can't get back?"

"Oh no," Viola said softly. "This won't do."

She turned away from us and leaned her head on the mantel above the fireplace. I thought I saw her shoulders shaking.

"I understand missing your father," she said, still facing the wall. "As a child, I missed my father, too. You see, he was a soldier and never came back from the war. I was only a child when he left. I never saw him again. My younger brother, Eddie, never even got to meet him."

Luna walked over and put her arms around Viola. She's a hugger, that Luna.

"And then, while still a young woman, I lost my son, David," Viola said, her voice trembling. "You can't imagine how much I miss him. It's been a lifetime since I've seen him."

She sounded so sad, I was almost tempted to join in the hug, which is saying a lot, because I'm not a hugger.

"We will help you find him next week," I said to Viola. "We promise."

She turned to me and smiled a little, but I could tell from the way her chin was shaking that she was trying not to cry.

"I feel him inside this painting, Tiger,"

she said. "As I worked on it, I felt I could see my David sitting at that counter, eating a slice of blueberry pie. I could almost hear his laughter."

I stared hard at the *Nighthawks* painting. New York City at night looked like a scary place. There wasn't a soul on the streets. There were only three customers in the diner. The man in the gray hat and the woman in the red dress looked so unhappy. And the guy sitting across from them was all hunched up like a bad guy in a movie. You couldn't see his face, but I imagined he had a big scar running down his cheek. I shivered a little. I wouldn't want to be David, wandering around those empty, dark streets.

But there was nothing we could do to

help him. Luna had to stay home and see her dad. And any minute now, my dad was going to come looking for me to start my report.

"Mrs. Dots," I said. "We want to help you and David. We really do but—"

Suddenly, we heard a loud crash coming from the other room. It was followed by a high-pitched squeal. That was definitely the sound of a pig!

"Help!" Chives cried. "I've lost control of the vehicle!"

"Don't tell me he's on that contraption of yours!" Viola said. "Who gave him permission to ride it?"

"I guess I did," I said. "He asked so nicely."

"That was a mistake," she snapped.

"Chives is a very clumsy pig. He can't do anything with those hooves."

"I'll go help him," Luna said.

But before she could leave, Chives came speeding in on the Snack 'N' Scoot.

His tie was caught on the handlebars, and his porky body was hanging off the side of the scooter. One of his back legs was stuck inside the cooler.

He must have tried to stop his fall by grabbing the red curtains. A large piece of velvet had torn off and was wrapped around his shoulders like Luna's Moon Girl cape. He was heading right toward the *Nighthawks* painting.

"Help!" he squealed again. "I can't stop this thing."

"Drag your feet along the floor!" I hollered out to him.

"I don't have feet," he hollered back. "I have hooves and they make very poor brakes."

"Hang on, Chives," Luna called. "Tiger

and I will stop you."

She grabbed my hand, and we formed a human wall in front of the painting.

"He's going to crash into us," she said. "Put your arms out to stop him!"

Bang! Boom! Crash!

Chives rode right into us. He flew into the air and landed with a thud on the floor. His cape got all tangled up in Luna's cape, but at least he didn't seem badly hurt.

I reached for the Snack 'N' Scoot to stop the wheels from spinning.

Just then, I heard a low rumble, like a train was going through a tunnel under the house. I felt the floor shake beneath my feet. A cold night wind blew into my face, and I thought I could smell hot coffee brewing. Or was it hot dogs? Or blueberry pie? Or was it all three?

I heard the clock on the frame strike its first chime, and I began to feel dizzy. The room spun in circles. The air felt electric, like it was vibrating. Then I heard a ripping sound, growing louder and louder until it almost seemed to fill the room. I squinted at the painting and saw a hole as big as my head opening up. I could feel myself being pulled in.

I was knocked off my feet. There was no use fighting. An invisible force was dragging my body closer and closer to the hole.

"Tiger!" I heard Luna scream. "Don't go! Don't go!"

But it was too late. The force from inside

the painting was too strong for me.

Down, down, down the tunnel I fell. Past tall skyscrapers. Past dark streets lined with old-fashioned cars. Past something that looked like the Statue of Liberty. I could hear my Snack 'N' Scoot thumping behind me, bouncing against soft walls, then whipping through the cold air.

Finally, I landed with a thud on concrete pavement. Ow, that hurt!

I peered into the darkness. Instantly, I knew where I was. It was the street in the painting. A bright yellow light from inside the diner gave the sidewalk an eerie green glow.

The night was full of shadows. And I was alone. All alone.

CHAPTER 4

I was shivering. It was really cold outside.

I blinked hard, trying to get my eyes to focus. What I saw was a dark and lonely city street. Maggie's pink princess scooter was the only splotch of color.

Wait! Was that a voice calling out to me?

"Tiger! Tiger! I'm coming!"

It was Luna. I couldn't see her, but I could hear her voice echo all around me. I looked up in the sky just in time to see her tumbling through the air.

I jumped to my feet and held my arms out. Luna crash-landed right on top of me and knocked me back down to the sidewalk.

"Why are you here?" I asked as I tried to sit up. "You weren't supposed to come."

"When I saw you get pulled into the painting, I got so afraid for you. I couldn't let you go alone. So I left Chives on the floor and jumped into the hole just before it closed up."

"But what about your dad?"

"We'll have to promise each other to get out on time," Luna said, "whether or not we find David. Is that a deal?"

I nodded and we shook hands. Luna stood up and brushed off her cape.

"Viola was sure David's somewhere in the diner," I said. "Let's go inside and find him."

"One little problem," Luna answered. "There's no door."

She was right. There was no door to the restaurant. But there were three customers inside and the guy who worked there. They had to have gotten in somehow.

"Maybe there's a secret door," Luna said, "that opens when you say a magic word."

I leaned the Snack 'N' Scoot against the window and followed Luna along the sidewalk. We pushed on the green tiles, saying "abracadabra" and "hocus-pocus." Nothing happened.

At last, we found a glass door that led into the lobby of a building. We crept inside. At the far end of the dark lobby, we could barely make out a narrow wooden door. We raced over, pushed it open, and found ourselves in a small kitchen. On the opposite wall was another wooden door with a window in it. We could see the yellow light from the diner shining through the window.

"That must be the way in," I whispered to Luna. "You ready to go inside?"

"Moon Girl was born ready," she said with a swish of her cape.

When we stuck our heads inside the diner, not one of the three customers even looked up. They sat there in complete silence. It wasn't what you'd call a friendly

place. Only the guy working behind the
counter smiled.

"Hello, folks," he said. "Come on in and
grab a stool. We've got hot coffee and some
swell blueberry pie."

Blueberry pie! That's exactly what Viola imagined David was eating, I thought.

"My name is Raymond, but everyone calls me Ray," he said, adjusting his white cap. "Can I cut you a slice of pie? Pretty rare to get real pie these days, what with the sugar ration and all."

"What's a sugar ration?" I asked as I slid onto one of the polished wooden stools.

"You're kidding me," Ray said. "You haven't heard? Each family gets a book of stamps. Every time you buy sugar, you've got to hand in a stamp. That's because it's in short supply. All the ships that carry sugar to the United States are being used for the war."

"That would be World War II, right?" I tried to sound casual, like I knew what I was talking about. I remembered Viola saying that *Nighthawks* was painted during World War II.

Ray gave me a strange look.

"Of course it's World War II, for Pete's sake. Where are you kiddos from, anyway?"

Luna walked over to the counter. As she stood in the yellow light of the diner, the bright *M* on her cape seemed to sparkle. Ray stared at it.

"You probably won't believe this, Ray," she said, "but we're from the future. I'm Luna, Moon Girl."

She spun around and her cape formed a circle in the air.

"Right. And I bet you're going to tell me you're the star of a comic book." Ray snickered. "Like Wonder Woman."

"Moon Girl's not a comic book hero," I

said. "She's the real thing."

Ray laughed again. But then, as he watched Luna spin around and around, his smile disappeared.

"How'd you get here, anyway?" he asked Luna.

"I flew," she answered. "Right through the air, across seventy-five years, and onto your sidewalk."

Ray looked over at me. "She's pulling my leg, right?" he said.

"It's all true," I answered.

"Holy applesauce," Ray said, swallowing hard.

Luna looked like she was about to confess that she wasn't really a superhero when I put my hand up and stopped her. I had an idea.

"I'll tell you what, Ray," I said. "I'll get Moon Girl to show you how she can fly if you help us out."

Luna caught on right away to what I was doing.

"We're looking for a person named David," she said. "He's about thirteen years old, brown hair, really nice guy. We've been told he's here in your painting . . . I mean . . . your diner."

"Are you talking about David Dots?" Ray asked. "That kid's been hanging around here a lot the last week or so."

"David Dots! Yes! That's the one!"

"He's a swell kid," Ray said. "Sometimes we play music together. I play bebop on the saxophone. David's taught me some swinging songs by a band called . . . um . . . the

49

Cockroaches, or some other kind of bug."

"You mean the Beatles?" Luna asked.

"That's it! How'd you know that?"

"They're from the future, too," Luna said.

Ray's eyebrows shot up. I think he was actually starting to believe that Luna was a superhero.

"Listen, Ray," I said. "David's mother is looking for him. We need to find him fast."

"He left a few minutes ago," Ray said.

"Oh no!" There was a little panic in Luna's voice. "Where did he go?"

"I sent him to my apartment," Ray said. "My aunt Janet lives with us, and she's having a baby. She called and said she needed to get to the hospital right away. My mom works nights at the navy yard in Brooklyn. Aunt Janet said she needed me to come babysit her three-year-old daughter. I told her I had to work here until nine o'clock closing time or the boss will fire me. So David said he'd go."

"Is your apartment far away?" Luna asked.

"Not for you," Ray said. "If you're really a superhero, you could fly there in about ten seconds."

"What if I can't fly right now?" Luna asked.

"You could take the subway," Ray said. "You want me to draw you a map?"

"Yes, please," I answered. "And fast!"

He pulled a pencil from behind his ear and grabbed a paper napkin.

"When you leave here, walk a few blocks to the subway," he said as he wrote. "Go down the stairs. Take the F train four stops to Delancey Street on the Lower East Side.

My apartment is on Essex Street, right above the bakery. But honestly, it'd be easier if you fly."

"Thanks, Ray. I'll discuss that with my cape," Luna said, grabbing the napkin map and heading for the door.

"Hey, Moon Girl, what about that flying demonstration?" Ray shouted after her.

"She'll give it to you when we come back here with David," I said.

"Jeepers, that will be swell. I'll have some pie waiting."

But Luna didn't hear a word he said. She was already out the door, heading into the dark streets of New York City.

CHAPTER 5

This was not the New York City I had seen in pictures. There were no skyscrapers poking up into the sky. No yellow taxicabs clogging up the streets. What we saw looked more like a dark, empty village. Brown and redbrick buildings filled both sides of the narrow street.

I grabbed the Snack 'N' Scoot and rode behind Luna. The streetlights cast long, dark shadows on the sidewalk. They looked like skinny zombies.

   Tiger!

I thought to myself.

Do not even think about zombies. Don't think of ghosts, either. Or vampires. Just keep your mind on scooting.

   After three blocks, we saw the subway entrance. It was a metal stairway with two round lights above it. We hurried over to it grabbed the Snack 'N' Scoot, and ran down the stairs.

It felt weird to go down into the subway station. I had never been underground before. Everyone else was standing around like it was a totally normal place to be. We didn't know where to go. We looked on the wall for signs, but all we saw were a bunch of posters of a woman called Miss Subways.

MEET MISS SUBWAYS

Lovely AMANDA LEE

Amanda lives in Brooklyn - interested in advertising - writes novels full of prose as attractive as its author.

"I wonder how we catch the F train, whatever that is," Luna said.

"There's a guard. I'll ask him."

"Okay. Be sure to tell him we're in a big hurry."

The man was wearing a blue jacket with gold buttons.

"Excuse me, sir," I said. "My friend and I are trying to get to Essex Street on the Lower East Side. We've never been in a subway before. Can you help us?"

"What? Never been in the New York subway?" he boomed. "Why, son, this is the finest subway system in the world. Open twenty-four hours a day, every day of the year."

"Yes, sir. We're in a hurry, so if I could just ask you . . ."

"Did you know that there are 660 miles of track in the New York subway?" he went on. "That's long enough to stretch from here to Chicago, Illinois."

"Yes, sir, that's very interesting, but . . ."

"Did I mention this here is the largest rapid transit system in the world?" There was no stopping him now. He was on a roll. "The first underground line started way back in 1904."

I had no idea how to get him to stop talking.

"Could you please just tell me where we catch the F train to Delancey Street?" I asked, trying to sound as grown-up as I could—which isn't very.

Luna could see that I needed help, so she came running over to us.

"Oh, who do we have here?" the guard asked, noticing her red cape. "Little Red Riding Hood? You on your way to Grandma's house?"

He let out a big laugh that bounced all around the subway tunnel. Luna stood up straight and gave him her most serious look. She doesn't like to be teased.

"Sir," she said. "There is a baby about to be born who needs our help. But if we don't get on that train right away, it may be too late."

Her serious face worked. The guard stopped laughing immediately.

"Go over to that turnstile," he said. "Drop in a token each and wait on the southbound platform until you see the F train. Hop on, go four stops, and you're there."

He was still talking as we grabbed the Snack 'N' Scoot and ran across the station. Luckily, I had some of my allowance money stuffed into my pocket. I dug out two nickels and bought the tokens just as I heard the train approach. Luna and I dashed to the turnstile, inserted the tokens, and ran through it and down the stairs to the platform.

"I know what to do when the train pulls to a stop and the doors open—jump inside! I've seen people do that in movies," I told Luna.

"You go first," she said.

The train came to a screeching stop right in front of us. The doors opened and a crowd of people got out all at once.

"You go first," Luna said, giving me a little shove.

I pushed my way through the crowd and lifted up the scooter to make sure the back wheel didn't get caught.

Once I was on board, I turned to check on Luna. She wasn't there!

I whipped around just in time to see the doors closing. Wait! There was something caught in them. It was a cape, a red cape.

"Luna!" I yelled. "Get inside!"

It was too late. The doors had slammed shut, with her cape caught in between them.

I could see her through the window of the train. She was outside, tugging on her cape, trying to get it unstuck. She was pulling as hard as she could.

Just as the train began to take off, she gave a mighty tug and her cape came free. She fell backward, away from the train. The last I saw of her, she was sitting on the floor of the station. I could hear her calling, "Tiger! Tiger!"

Luna never sounds scared, but she did then. And I didn't blame her. I was speeding away, leaving her all alone in the belly of a big, strange city.

CHAPTER 6

The train raced through the dark tunnel, taking me farther and farther away from Luna. I thought how frightened she must be. Then I realized my heart was beating fast. I was scared, too.

I wanted to ask someone for help, but I wasn't sure who to ask. I decided to take a chance and ask the man standing closest to me.

I tapped him on the shoulder. He turned around and frowned at me. A gray hat

covered one eye and cast a shadow on his face.

"What do you want, kid?" he growled in a mean voice. I tried to stay calm, but my words got all mixed up.

"I was wondering how to get off the subway," I said. "I mean . . . when to get off. I mean . . . if I should get off."

He squinted his beady eyes at me.

"Listen, pip-squeak," he said. "I don't know where you're from, but it sure ain't here. It's not hard. The doors open. You get out. End of story."

Well, that was clear. It wasn't nice, but it was clear.

The minute the doors opened, I grabbed my Snack 'N' Scoot and dashed out of the train. I was in another station that looked a lot like the one we had just left.

"Hey, little soldier," a voice said. "I like your jeep. Never seen a pink two-wheeler before."

It was a man in an army uniform. He looked like this picture we have of my grandpa when he was in the army. He even had a bunch of medals on his chest.

"You AWOL?" he asked me.

"I might be," I said, "if I knew what that meant."

"Army talk," he said. "It means *absent without leave*. You know, like when you sneak away without permission."

"Oh, then I definitely am," I said. "I'm looking for my friend. She's AWOL, too. I need to get back to the station I just came from."

"Easy as pie. You go over there across the tracks," he said. "Good luck."

I put my hand up to my forehead and saluted. I saw that in a movie once.

The soldier laughed and saluted back. He seemed so nice. I hoped he was going to be safe in the war.

I had to wait almost five minutes for the train. I checked the clock on the subway wall. We had already used up seventeen minutes of the hour of power, and we hadn't even come close to finding David yet.

The F train pulled up and I got on. When

the doors opened at the next stop, I jumped off. I raced to the southbound platform.

There was no Luna in sight. Panicked, I shouted her name, which echoed across the station.

"Luna!" I called. "Luna, are you here?"

There was no answer—only a strange, terrible moan, like a donkey with a bad stomachache. *What was that sound? And where is Luna?* I thought.

My eyes darted around the station. I could feel the minutes slipping away.

Over in a corner, I noticed a small crowd had gathered. I thought I caught a glimpse of something red in the middle of it. I bolted across the station and pushed my way through the people. There, in the middle of the crowd, was Luna!

Sitting on a chair next to her was a man with a saw between his knees. A real saw, like the kind you saw wood with. He held the end of it with one hand, and with the other one, pulled a violin bow across the saw's jagged edge. So that was where the awful noise was coming from.

"Tiger!" Luna called out when she saw me.

The man stopped playing. Luna threw her arms around me—the kind of hug I call the Luna Special. Normally, I'm not a big fan of the Luna Special, but if it kept that man from playing his saw, I was all for it.

"I've been calling for you!" I told her.

"It's hard to hear anything over Sammy's playing," she said. "Tiger, this is my new friend, Sammy Sampson. He invented the singing saw. Isn't it great?"

"The greatest," I lied.

I never would have told him the truth—that if I heard one more note from his saw, my ears would jump off my head and run away to the North Pole. I know that when you invent something, it really hurts your feelings if people don't like it.

"You're not going to believe this. Sammy lives on Essex Street. It's his neighborhood."

"When you kids get there, say hi to my pal Willie," Sammy said. "And Ethel. And Gino and Paula, too."

"We will," I said, even though I had no idea who any of those people were. All I knew was that we had to get moving fast.

Luna said a quick good-bye, and we caught the next train. After four stops, we got off and rushed up the stairs to the street. It was dark, but I could see that the sign said Delancey Street.

"I'm not the best reader in the world," I said, "but that doesn't look like it says Essex Street to me."

"Sammy said you walk down Delancey past Willie's Kitchen and poof, you're on Essex."

We walked really fast. The lights from the windows of the buildings cast weird shadows on the sidewalk.

These are not zombies, Tiger, I said to myself. I admit it. I said it more than once. I might even have said it six times. Okay, it was eight to be exact.

Suddenly, I saw a human-shaped shadow lurch out of a doorway and move toward us.

"Help!" I screamed. I was so scared,

I must have jumped five feet in the air.

"Don't be afraid, kid. It's just me, Willie."

"Willie!" Luna said. "Are you Sammy Sampson's friend?"

"Yup, Sammy and me, we're thick as mud. Two peas in a pod."

"He's my friend, too," Luna told him.

"How about if I fry you kids up a couple of burgers?" Willie offered. "Any friend of Sammy's is a friend of mine."

"Thanks, Willie, but we're in a huge hurry," Luna said.

"How about some hot dogs?" Willie asked. Before we could answer, he called to a man pushing a cart.

"Hey, Gino!" he shouted. "You got any red hot dogs and cold drinks left in there?"

"Coming right up," Gino answered.

"This is really nice of you, Gino, but we don't have time to eat," I said.

"Take them to go, kids. Live it up," Gino said, handing us the food.

"Great idea," Luna said. "Let's put them in the Snack 'N' Scoot. I'll bring them to the fiesta." Turning to Willie, she explained, "My dad's in the army. He's coming home on leave tonight, and we're giving him a party."

A woman in a puffy green coat hurried over, pushing another cart. "We love our soldiers," she said. "How about I send them some hot pretzels? Extra mustard, no charge."

"That's my Ethel," Gino said. "And I'll go inside and get Paula to throw in some pickles, too. Dill and half-sour."

Before you could say "Sammy Sampson and his singing saw," the cooler on my Snack 'N' Scoot was full of New York treats for us to take home.

That was the good news. The bad news was that we had to run the rest of the block to Essex Street dragging the Snack 'N' Scoot behind us. It was much heavier now that it was loaded with food. I made a mental note to do something about that when I got home. An inventor's work is never done.

At the corner of Essex and Delancey, we saw a Chinese restaurant. Next to it was a small bakery.

"That's the building," I said. "Let's go find David."

"Tiger, do you really think we have enough time to find him and get back to the diner?" Luna asked.

"Sure," I said. "No problem."

But we both knew that wasn't true. The clock was ticking, and we were running out of time.

CHAPTER 7

All Ray had told us was that his aunt lived above the bakery. He forgot to mention on what floor. There was a metal balcony on each floor, connected by a long metal ladder.

"Hey, kid, why are you staring at my fire escape?" A man in a white apron had popped out of the shadows and was suddenly standing in front of us. He had flour all over his hands.

"Fire escape? Is that what you call that ladder thing?" I asked.

"Where are you from? Mars?" He snorted. "Never seen a fire escape before?"

"We're looking for Aunt Janet's apartment," Luna said.

"I don't know any Aunt Janet," he said. "I got an Aunt Shirley, but she's upstairs soaking her false teeth in a glass of water. This Aunt Janet, she got a last name?"

"I'm sure she does," I said. "But we don't know it. She has a nephew named Ray. And a three-year-old daughter."

"Oh, I know who you're talking about," the baker said. "That little girl's got some mouth on her. They live on the top floor."

"Where's the elevator?" I asked.

"It's called your feet," the baker said. "These apartments are all walk-ups."

Luna picked up the front end of the Snack 'N' Scoot. I picked up the back.

"On your mark, get set, go!" she said.

By the time we raced up to the top floor, I could hardly breathe. There were four apartments on the floor.

"Which one do you think is Ray's?" Luna asked.

I walked over to one of the doors and

leaned my ear up against it. It was silent inside. Then I went to another door and listened. I heard someone singing.

"He's in there," I said. "That's David."

"How do you know?" Luna asked.

"Because he's singing 'I Want to Hold Your Hand,'" I said. "It's a Beatles song my grandma always sings. It wasn't even written in 1942. You would have to be from the future to know that song."

Suddenly, I heard a little girl's voice coming from inside the apartment. At least I thought it was a little girl's voice. Either that or a wicked witch.

"Stop singing!" the girl screamed. "You're making my ears hurt."

I heard David say something to her, which made her scream even louder.

"I want my mommy, not you!" she yelled.

"Sounds like David could use some help," Luna said.

She knocked on the door.

"Who's there?"

"Surprise visitors from the future!" Luna yelled back.

The door flew open and there was David Dots, standing in front of us. He was wearing pants that came just below his knee, and long colorful socks. He threw his arms around us in a huge group hug.

"Come in," he said. "I assume my mother sent you. But

how'd you find me here?"

"Ray told us where you were," I said.

"That Ray, he's a swell guy," David said.

"He's got you wearing some crazy pants and talking like him, too," I said.

"Yeah, he's teaching me to talk like all the fellows. They say cool things like *jeepers* and *holy applesauce* and *gee willikers*. Did he tell you he lets me play piano in his band? We've been jamming together ever since I got here."

"How long have you been here, David?" Luna asked.

"I'm not sure," he said. "In the world of art, time doesn't really matter. I'm having a fantastic time. New York is great, except for the war. Lots of the fellows have dads who are fighting overseas."

"Your mom told us about that," I said.

"How is she?" David asked.

"She misses you so much," Luna said. "We came to take you home. The hour of power ends at five. Will you come with us this time?"

Before David could answer, the little girl let out another loud scream.

"I don't like you people," she shrieked. "I want my mommy!"

Luna bent down and took her hand. "Your mommy's at the hospital having a baby, *chiquita*. You're going to have a little brother or a little sister very soon."

"It better be a baby brother," she said. "Because I'm not sharing my dolls with a baby sister. Baby sisters stink."

I had to agree with the baker. This little

tot did have some mouth on her. Luna was sweet to her, though. She picked her up and put her on her lap.

"What would you like to call your baby brother?" she asked.

"I want to name him Eddie. Mommy promised me we could call him Eddie, and that's what we're going to call him."

"Eddie's a cool name," I said. "And what's your name?"

"Not telling," she answered. "I'm not talking to boys."

"She wouldn't tell me her name," David whispered. "And I'm the babysitter."

"You have to turn it into a game so she learns to trust you," Luna said. "My grandma taught me that. She's great with kids."

Turning to the little girl, Luna said, "I bet I can guess your name. Is it Puffy Pants?"

"No!" the little girl answered.

"Is it Pumpkin Head?"

The little girl was actually sort of smiling now.

"No!"

"I know!" Luna said. "It's Penny Picklebottom!"

The little girl burst out laughing.

"No, silly!" she said. "It's Viola! Viola Dots!"

The room suddenly went completely silent. No one knew what to say. We just sat there, letting it sink in. Finally, David spoke.

"Holy applesauce," he said, staring at the little girl in Luna's lap. "She's my mother."

CHAPTER 8

At first, I didn't believe it. It was impossible to imagine that the child sitting on Luna's lap was actually Viola Dots. But as we added up the clues, it made sense.

"This little girl is very grumpy," I began. "Just like Viola. No offense, David."

"That's okay," he said. "We all know my mother has a temper."

Luna added some clues of her own.

"Viola did say she was born in New York," she said. "And that her little brother

was named Eddie. David, was your grandmother's name Janet?"

"No, it was Jan. Grandma Jan."

"Jan as in Janet?"

"I see your point," David said.

"Don't forget that Viola also said her father fought in World War II," I mentioned.

"My daddy's in the army, too," the little girl chimed in. "Far away. I miss him. I'm going to see him soon."

Luna looked at little Viola. I saw tears fill her eyes. We both knew the truth. Viola was not going to see her father again.

"Your daddy will always be with you," Luna said to her softly. "Right here in your heart."

"I don't want him there," Viola shouted. "I want him here in my apartment. I'm going to find him right now."

She jumped off Luna's lap and ran into the bedroom.

"Do you guys know that my grandpa died in the war?" David said. "My uncle Eddie never even got to meet him."

"We know," Luna said. "It's so sad."

"Poor little Viola." David glanced into the bedroom. "I'm going to go see if I can cheer her up."

"Big Viola could really use some cheering up, too," I said.

"Your mother loves you very much," Luna whispered to him.

David smiled, as if he were remembering happy times from the past.

"I love her, too," he said. "Lately, I've missed her a lot."

"Then come home with us," I begged. "If we hurry, we can get little Viola back to the diner. We'll give her to Ray, and then you can get into the painting with us."

"Okay," he said at last. "I'll come with you. It's time I came home." He smiled. "I just hope she remembers how to make that delicious French toast."

David hurried into the bedroom to find Viola. I checked the clock on the kitchen wall. We had exactly eighteen minutes left until the hour of power ended. If everything went right, we just might make it back.

"Oh no!" I heard David shout from the bedroom. "She's gone!"

Luna and I dashed for the bedroom. David was on his knees, looking under the bed. I ran into the bathroom and searched behind the door and in the bathtub. No Viola.

"Look," Luna said. "The window's open. Where does that lead?"

"To the fire escape!" David answered.

The three of us ran to the window and looked out. There, curled up on the fire escape, five stories above the street, was little Viola Dots.

"Viola, come back in here right now,"

I said, using the

same voice I use to boss Maggie around.

"It's dangerous out there."

   "I'm not coming in until I get to see my

daddy."

David held his head in his hands. "I'm afraid if I climb out to get her, she'll try to get away and fall."

"Hey, what's going on up there?" came a voice from below. I poked my head out and saw the baker standing on the sidewalk, looking up.

"Go back inside, little girl!" he shouted. "Or I'm going to call the fire department."

"I don't care!" Viola shouted. "I'm not leaving here."

He disappeared inside the bakery. As the seconds ticked by, the three of us tried to think of some way to get her back inside.

"I have an idea," Luna said. "David, do you know if they have any art supplies in this apartment?"

"I don't know," he answered. "There's a

desk in the living room."

Luna ran into the living room, returning with a drawing pad and some crayons.

"What's that for?" I asked.

"Well, what is the one thing we know about Viola Dots?"

"That she's a good artist," I answered right away.

"And I'll bet she loved art even as a little girl," Luna said. "I'm going to go out there and draw with her. If I can get her to trust me, maybe she'll come inside."

"But, Luna, that could take forever," I said. "We barely have fifteen minutes to get back to the diner. Remember our promise, to get you back to your dad no matter what?"

"Tiger, we can't leave Viola out there. Anything could happen to her."

Luna climbed through the open window and out onto the fire escape.

"Hi, *chiquita*," she said to Viola. "I brought you some crayons. Do you want to draw with me?"

Luna sat down on the fire escape next to Viola. She handed her crayons as Viola drew a picture of a man with black curly hair in what looked like a brown uniform.

"Is that your daddy?" Luna asked.

"Yes," Viola said. "Now I can always have him with me."

I heard a siren coming down the street. I ran to the living room window and poked my head out far enough to see an old fire truck pull up in front of the bakery. Well, it looked old to me, but it was probably new in 1942.

A firefighter in a
black helmet got out
of the truck and looked
at the fire escape. He took a
loudspeaker from his truck
and called up to Viola.

"You just stay where you
are, honey, and we'll come get
you."

I ran back into the bedroom to see how I
could help.

"I'm not going with that man," Viola was
shouting. "I won't!"

"I understand," Luna said softly. "I have
another idea. Let's take the beautiful picture
you made of your daddy and put it up on
the refrigerator. Would you like to do that?"

"Yes," said Viola. "I'd like that a lot."

Luna stood up, balancing carefully on the narrow metal fire escape. I held my breath as she turned around in the little space.

Be careful, Luna, I thought. *Be very careful.*

She bent down and picked up Viola. Inch by inch, she crept toward the open window. David and I each held out a hand and helped them inside.

"Thank you," David said to Luna.

"For what?" she asked.

"For saving my mother's life," he whispered.

Luna held on to little Viola with one arm and put her other arm out to David. I think we all know what happened next. That's right, a huge Luna Special.

CHAPTER 9

David helped Viola tape the picture of her daddy up on the refrigerator.

"I like you now," she told him. "Maybe I'll let you be my babysitter."

"I'm glad you like me," David said.

"Good. Then let's have a pretend tea party."

"David doesn't have time for a tea party," Luna said, looking up at the kitchen clock. We were now down to less than ten minutes to get to the diner.

"We'll never make it to the diner by five,"
David said.

"We have to try," I said. "David, you carry your mother . . . I mean . . . Viola. Luna and I will take the Snack 'N' Scoot. Let's see how fast we can get downstairs."

We made it downstairs in record time. When I pushed open the front door, I ran smack into the baker. The minute Viola saw him, she started to scream. And when I say scream, I mean S-C-R-E-A-M!

"It's okay," Luna whispered to her. "He's a nice man."

"No, he's not," wailed Viola.

She said some other stuff, too, but we

couldn't understand the words. All we could really hear was *wah-wah-wah-wah-waaaaaaaaaah*. She was having a full-out tantrum. I thought Maggie's were bad, but this one was a prizewinner.

"Viola, can you use your inside voice?" Luna suggested.

That made her wail even louder.

"I don't know how to get her to stop," Luna said. "Can you think of something?"

I had only one thought in my mind. It was *ticktock, ticktock*.

"I have an idea," David said. He walked up to the firefighter, who was just getting back into his fire truck.

"We have to get someplace really fast, and as you can see, we have a very upset little girl. I was thinking that maybe a ride on a fire truck would calm her down," he said.

"We're not in the habit of taking kids on rides," the firefighter answered, climbing aboard his truck.

When Viola heard that, she started to scream even louder, if that was possible.

"I want to go for a ride on that truck," she shrieked in between sobs. "If I don't get to go, I'm going to cry and cry until forever."

"I believe her," the baker said, putting his flour-covered hands over his ears. "And I can't take this."

"Please," I said to the firefighter. "This little girl's cousin works at a diner not too far away. If you could take us there, maybe he can get her to stop crying."

"Viola, wouldn't you like to go see cousin Ray?" Luna said. She had to talk very loudly to be heard over the sobs. Viola was crying so hard, she had given herself the hiccups.

"Ray!" she hiccupped. "I—*hic*—like—*hic*—cousin—*hic*—Ray!"

"Come on, be a swell guy and help us out," David said to the fireman.

"For this poor little girl's sake," I added. I thought that had a nice ring to it.

"Okay, I'll do it for my ears' sake," the fireman said. "And the baker's. This is where I get my buttered roll each morning. I want him to be able to hear my order."

We jumped in the back of the fire truck before he could change his mind.

"Where, exactly, is this diner?" the fireman called back to us.

"Greenwich Village," David said.

"I may regret this, but hold on."

He flipped on the siren and took off.

David held Viola as we raced through the streets of New York. Just like I'd thought, her wails turned into laughter and shrieks of joy. She snuggled up between us as the cold wind whipped at our faces. It was the most fun ride I'd ever had.

And to top it off, I got to see the Statue of Liberty. It was just a glimpse as we turned a corner, but there she was, standing in the middle of the New York harbor. As Ray would say, that was really swell.

We pulled up to the diner and jumped out quickly.

"What time is it?" I shouted to the firefighter.

"Time for me to get back to the station," he yelled as he drove off.

We looked in the window of the diner. Ray was behind the counter. The man and woman customers were sitting silently next to each other. The man with his back to us was still hunched over his coffee. Yellow light poured out the window, onto the shadowy street.

"We've got three minutes," David said, checking his watch.

"That's just enough time to give Viola to Ray and get back into the painting," I said.

"On your mark, get set, go!" Luna said.

We sprang into action. I parked the Snack 'N' Scoot on the sidewalk where we had landed, and the three of us raced in through the secret door. When we burst into the diner, Ray was glad to see us.

"Moon Girl!" he said. "I got your blueberry pie right here."

"Thanks, Ray," Luna said. "I'm going to take it with me in my superpowered superhero vehicle."

David handed Viola over to Ray. She was happy to see him.

"I love you, cousin Ray," she said,

snuggling in his arms.

"It's time for me to say good-bye," David said to Ray. "You keep an eye on little Viola. Make sure she grows up okay."

"Where are you going, kiddo?" Ray asked.

"Home."

David took a long look out the window of the diner. "So long, New York," he said. "It's been swell."

We hurried outside. Ray followed us, bouncing Viola in his arms.

"Can I watch you take off?" he asked. "You said I could see Moon Girl fly."

"Okay, but you need to be on that side of the street," I told him. I pointed to a building that was not in the painting.

I sat down on the sidewalk near the

Snack 'N' Scoot. Luna took her place next to me.

"Huddle up with us," I told David. "And be prepared to time travel."

David scrunched down on the sidewalk next to us.

We waited. Nothing happened. No rumble. No ripping. Just silence.

"Why aren't we taking off?" I asked.

"I don't know," Luna said. "Everything is the same in the painting as when we arrived."

"No, it's not. It's Ray. He's not behind the counter. It won't work unless everything is exactly the same," I replied.

A clock chimed in the distance. Oh no! The hour of power was here.

"Leave this to me," David said. He

jumped to his feet and ran across the street to Ray. "Give me Viola!" he commanded. "You hurry inside and stand behind the counter."

"Why?" Ray asked. "What's going on?"

"Just do it," David told him. As he took Viola in his arms, he yelled to us, "Tell my mother I had to stay here to take care of her. Otherwise, I might never have been born."

"No, David!" I screamed.

"There's no other way. Travel safely!"

Ray ran inside and took his place behind the counter just as the clock chimed again. The ground started to rumble beneath us. The ripping sound grew louder and louder. I heard David calling good-bye.

And that was the last thing I remember.

CHAPTER 10

Luna and I were tumbling through time and space. Cloudy, dark images of tall buildings, old cars, and the Statue of Liberty flashed in front of my eyes. I heard Luna calling my name, and the *thunk, thunk, thunk* of my Snack 'N' Scoot bumping against an invisible wall.

Suddenly, I saw the back of the canvas approaching at lightning speed. We shot through the hole in the painting and found ourselves in Viola's living room, sprawled on the shiny wooden floor. I was looking directly into her face. Chives was staring at me, too. He had a bandage over one eye and his arm in a sling.

As I started to sit up, I was knocked back down by the Snack 'N' Scoot bonking me in the head. Amazingly, it was still in one piece.

"Is this contraption all you brought back?" Viola asked. "Where is David?"

"We had him," Luna told her. "He was on his way back with us. He said he loves you, and he really wants to come home."

"Then why isn't he here?"

"He had to babysit," I answered.

"Nonsense!" Viola looked hurt. "Why would he choose to take care of a stranger's child when he could return home and take care of his own mother?"

"He *is* taking care of you, in his own way," I said.

Viola shook her head.

"You're speaking in riddles," she said angrily. "You're going to have to learn to express yourself more clearly."

"Yes, ma'am," I said. "I'll try harder next time."

"And when will next time be?" she asked us. "Tomorrow?"

"No," Luna told her. "My papa is coming home for the weekend."

"And I have a big report to write," I said.

"It seems I have no choice. I'll just have to wait for you to return." Viola sighed impatiently. "I suppose it will give me time to do a new painting. Chives, show the children out. And for goodness' sake, stay off that vehicle. I'm not your nurse. I don't want to have to bandage you up again."

We picked up the Snack 'N' Scoot and followed Chives to the door.

"I do apologize for her temper," he said.

"We understand," I said. "Luna and I know she's had a hard life."

"How do you know that?" he asked.

Luna and I shot each other a secret glance.

"Just a feeling," we both said at once.

We told Chives we'd see him soon and hurried out. We jumped on the Snack 'N' Scoot and rode it back to our duplex. My dad was waiting outside. Even though he looked angry, I was so glad to see him. I thought of Viola's dad and realized that

I was lucky to have my dad, safe at home
with all of us.

"Where have you been, Tiger?" he asked.

Luna answered for me.

"Don't be upset with him, Mr. Brooks,"
she said. "My papa is coming home tonight,
and Tiger offered to help me get some food
for our fiesta. We got hot dogs and pretzels

and pickles and even blueberry pie."

"That's a tasty menu," my dad said. "I'm glad Tiger offered to help."

"My grandma always makes her special sweet tamales for fiestas," Luna went on. "Maybe your whole family can come. I know my papa would love to meet you."

"That's a lovely invitation, Luna," my dad said. "We'd be happy to come."

I took the cooler off the scooter and helped Luna carry it upstairs. When I came back, I returned the scooter to Maggie.

"You better not have ruined it," she said. "Does it still have magical powers?"

"Very magical," I said. "It can travel through time."

Maggie gave me a disgusted look, the way little sisters do.

"You say the stupidest things, Tiger," she said.

Everyone had a great time at the fiesta. I met Luna's father and gave him my best salute. He laughed and saluted back. Luna and I shared one of Gino's hot dogs. It was great. No, make that swell. I didn't even mind when my dad made me write my transportation report afterward. It was easy. And I'll bet you know why.

That's right. It was on the New York subway system.

Ms. Warner said it was outstanding, so real that you would think I had been there myself. I got an A and she said it was the best in the class.

Thank you, fantastic frame!

ABOUT THE PAINTING

Nighthawks by Edward Hopper

Nighthawks, by Edward Hopper, is one of the most famous paintings in all of American art. The painting was completed in 1942, soon after America entered World War II. It shows "a restaurant on New York's Greenwich Avenue where two streets meet." It is typical of a style called American Realism, which aimed to show real people in their everyday lives.

Nighthawks is a painting of an all-night diner in which three customers are gathered. They are being served by a young man in a white hat. The three customers seem sad and lonely, lost in their own thoughts. Although they are sitting close to one another, no one is touching. We get the sense that they are separate and alone.

Unlike many paintings, *Nighthawks*

doesn't tell a story. It asks a thousand questions but doesn't give answers to any of them. Who are these people? Do they know one another? Why are they there? Is something about to happen? Did something just happen? How did they get inside? (There is no visible door outside.) The painting makes us feel that the four people are trapped inside the diner and we are outside, looking in. New York is all around them, but they are all alone in the big city.

What we notice the most about this beautiful painting is Edward Hopper's dramatic use of light and shadows. The bright yellow light pours out of the glass windows of the diner, casting weird shadows onto the dark city sidewalks. Our eyes are drawn to the fluorescent light inside the diner. Hopper forces our eyes to focus on the light and the shadows, and never on the details of the scene. Notice how few details or objects you can see in *Nighthawks*. Napkin holders, salt and pepper shakers, coffee mugs. Can you find the cash register in the store across the street? You have to look hard. It's hidden in the shadows.

Edward Hopper was born in 1882. He was raised in a town on the Hudson River in New York, and attended the New York School of Art. Until he became a famous painter, he worked as an illustrator in New York City. Being an illustrator helped form his painting style, which has a lot in common with photography. His paintings don't tell a whole story. They capture a moment in time, just like a photograph does. Their beauty comes from his ability to create a mood that fills us with emotion and awe.

Edward Hopper lived in New York City until he died in 1967. Even though he became one of the country's most famous artists, he continued to live in the same simple walk-up apartment all his life. He had to carry buckets of coal, which was used for heat, up four flights of stairs. He and his wife shared a bathroom with other people on the same floor. Hopper was a quiet man. Perhaps that explains why most of the people and places in his paintings focus on calm, silent subject matter.

Nighthawks is painted in oil on canvas. It is a large painting, five feet long and almost three feet high. As soon as Hopper finished it in January 1942, it became an instant classic. It was bought by the Art Institute of Chicago for $3,000. It has remained there ever since.

ABOUT THE AUTHOR

Lin Oliver is the *New York Times* best-selling author of more than thirty books for young readers. She is also a film and television producer, having created shows for Nickelodeon, PBS, Disney Channel, and Fox. The cofounder and executive director of the Society of Children's Book Writers and Illustrators, she loves to hang out with children's book creators. Lin lives in Los Angeles, in the shadow of the Hollywood sign, but when she travels, she visits the great paintings of the world and imagines what it would be like to be inside the painting—so you might say she carries her own fantastic frame with her!

ABOUT THE ILLUSTRATOR

Samantha Kallis is a Los Angeles–based illustrator and visual development artist. Since graduating from Art Center College of Design in Pasadena, California, in 2010, her work has been featured in television, film, publishing, and galleries throughout the world. Samantha can be found most days on the porch of her periwinkle-blue Victorian cottage, where she lives with her husband and their two cats. More of her work can be seen on her website: www.samkallis.com.